The Monster in the Cave

by
Nicholas Heller

GREENWILLOW BOOKS, New York

The full-color art was done
in ink and watercolor.

The typeface is Egyptian 505.

Library of Congress Cataloging-in-Publication Data

Heller, Nicholas.   The monster in the cave.
   Summary: Even though his parents and older
brother insist that monsters are not real,
Tobias hunts for a special Christmas gift
for the monster who lives in the cave.
   [1 Monsters—Fiction.   2. Christmas—Fiction]   I. Title.
PZ7.H37426Mo 1987   [E]   86-29598
ISBN 0-688-07313-1
ISBN 0-688-07314-X (lib. bdg.)

FOR PERNILLA

It was the day before Christmas,
and Tobias had a present for
almost everyone.

He had a strange machine for his father,

and an unusual hat for his mother.

There was a box of inflatable dinosaurs
for his brother,

and a lovely cactus
for his little sister.

But what could Tobias give to the monster who lived in the cave at the bottom of the hill?

Nothing seemed quite right.

So Tobias went to his father.
"What should I give the monster in
the cave for Christmas?" he asked.

"Why, Tobias," replied his father,
"you should know there are
no such things as monsters!"

So Tobias went to his mother.
"You know the monster in the cave at the
bottom of the hill?" he asked. "What do you
think I should give him for Christmas?"

But his mother said, "Why you silly boy,
there are no monsters in the cave.
There are no monsters anywhere.
Who gave you such an idea?"

Then Tobias asked his big brother, but his brother only
made fun of him. "Tobias, you're a dummy," he said.
"Everyone knows there are no such things as monsters."

Then his brother jumped around the room,
making silly monster noises and
waving his arms through the air.

Tobias went and sat at the bottom
of the staircase. After he had
been there for a while wondering what
to do, along came his little sister.

"What's the matter, Tobias?" she asked him.
Tobias explained about the monster, and how
he would like to give him a Christmas present.
"But no one even believes in him," said Tobias.

"Oh," said his sister, and she sat down on the
stairs with him. Then she jumped up again.
"We could bake him a cake," she said. "I'll help you."
"Do you think monsters like cake?" asked Tobias.
"Yes," said his sister. "I'm sure they do."

Late that night, while everyone
else was sleeping, Tobias and
his sister went downstairs
to the kitchen.

They took the biggest pan they could find and
filled it up with flour and eggs, milk and sugar,
chocolate, cinnamon, butter, and cream.

Then they added a few apples,
stirred it up,

and put it in the oven to bake.

After a while they took it out again.
"It's kind of a funny-looking cake,"
said Tobias doubtfully.
"But it's just right for a monster,"
replied his sister.

They wrapped it up and set off
down the hill to the cave.

There was the monster all by himself.
"A present for me?" he asked. "No one has ever
brought me a present before. How wonderful!"

"Why, it's a cake!" cried the monster.
"I just love cake, and I don't get
   to have it very often. You must stay
   and help me eat it."

So the three of them had a little party,
and the monster told Tobias and his sister
all about what it was like to be a monster,
and they all got very full of cake.

Then it was time for Tobias and his sister to go.
They said goodbye to the monster and promised
to come and visit him again soon.
They got home just in time for breakfast.

"Merry Christmas," said their mother. "Have you
two been out playing so early? You must be hungry.
Look, I've made you a big stack of pancakes!"
But Tobias and his sister were so full of cake
that they couldn't eat a bite.

"They are too excited," said their parents.
And they all gathered around the Christmas
tree to open their presents.